Karen's Big Fight

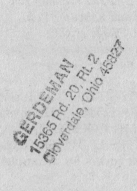

Little Sister

Karen's Big Fight
Ann M. Martin

Illustrations by Susan Tang

A
LITTLE APPLE
PAPERBACK

SCHOLASTIC INC.
New York Toronto London Auckland Sydney

ISBN 0-590-69187-2

12 11 10 9 8 7 6 5 4 3 2 1   6 7 8 9/9 0 1/0

Printed in the U.S.A.   40

First Scholastic printing, November 1996

The author gratefully acknowledges
Diane Molleson
for her help
with this book.

The Big House

"I love fall," I said to Moosie and Andrew. Moosie is my stuffed cat. He did not answer me. But my little brother Andrew did.

"Why?" he asked. He climbed up on a chair to look out my bedroom window.

"Because of the leaves — and Halloween, of course," I added.

"But Halloween is over," Andrew pointed out. "Does that mean fall is over?"

"No. Fall lasts until December twenty-first," I said. "Besides, as long as there are leaves on the ground, it is still fall."

"Oh," said Andrew. He is little enough to believe *almost* everything I tell him.

"You know, Andrew, it is November now," I said. (I do most of the talking when I am with Andrew.) "Do you know how I know that?"

"Because we are at the big house," Andrew answered. Our parents are divorced. We spend every other month with Daddy at the big house. The rest of the time we live with Mommy at the little house. (I will tell you more about my two houses later.)

"Karen, Andrew," Nannie called from downstairs. "I am making hot chocolate. Would you like some?"

"Sure!" we shouted. (Nannie is our step-grandmother. We love her a lot.)

"Nannie, can I have marshmallows in my hot chocolate?" I asked when we ran in the kitchen.

"Of course," Nannie answered.

"Say please, Karen," Daddy reminded me. Daddy is around during the day because he works at home. He sat at the big kitchen table with Emily Michelle. (Emily Michelle is one of my sisters. She is only two and a half.)

"Choo-choo!" Emily Michelle cried. (She was trying to say *chocolate*.)

"Yes, you may have some," Nannie answered.

"Mmm, something smells good in here," someone said. The kitchen door opened. I looked up and saw Kristy.

"You are home early," I said. I was very pleased to see her. Kristy is my stepsister. She is also one of my favorite people ever.

"You probably smell the pot roast we're having tonight," Nannie told Kristy.

"Or the hot chocolate," I added.

Kristy poured some hot chocolate into her favorite mug. (It is shaped like a baseball.) Then she sat down next to me. I was looking forward to telling her about my day at school when David Michael barged in the door. Boo and bullfrogs!

David Michael is one of my stepbrothers. He can be a real pest. In fact, he has been such a pest lately that we have not been getting along too well.

"How was Play-by-Play?" Daddy asked David Michael. Play-by-Play is an after-school club at David Michael's school. Kids put on plays and learn all about the theater. David Michael loves it.

"Great," answered David Michael. He squeezed his chair between Kristy and me. (See what I mean about being a pest?) "We're putting on *Winnie-the-Pooh*."

"Cool!" said Kristy.

"And you know what?" said David Michael. He made sure he had everyone's attention. "I am going to be Piglet."

"Piglet!" I squealed. "You are going to play a *pig*?" I could not stop laughing. David Michael gave me a dirty look.

"Congratulations!" said Daddy. He patted David Michael on the shoulder. "Piglet is a very big part. I am proud of you. I am also pleased your schoolwork has been improving lately."

David Michael beamed. (It was lucky for

4

him his schoolwork had been improving, or he probably could not be in the play at all. But Piglet?)

I was still chuckling, but everyone ignored me.

"To David Michael's new part," said Kristy. She held out her mug of hot chocolate.

"To David Michael," everyone said, except me.

November was going to be a *long* month.

2

A Long Dinner

I have a *big* family. Dinners at the big house always take a long time because there are so many of us, and everyone has so much to say.

David Michael told us — again — about playing Piglet in *Winnie-the-Pooh*.

"We know," I whispered to my napkin. But Kristy heard me.

"Karen," she whispered back, "not everyone has heard David Michael's news."

I nodded. Then I began giggling. I

thought about the costume David Michael would wear. Probably something shiny and pink with a snout. And I laughed even harder.

No one else was laughing. Elizabeth was telling David Michael how relieved she was that his schoolwork had been improving. "Oh, and I'm so proud of you for getting this *big* part," Elizabeth was saying. I rolled my eyes. (Elizabeth is David Michael's mother, my stepmother. She is usually pretty cool.)

Nannie said she would sew David Michael's costume. Kristy wanted to bring all her friends to watch his play.

I was happy when Elizabeth changed the subject. "David Michael," she began, "we have a surprise for you."

"You do?" asked David Michael. I sat up a little straighter. What could it be? I wondered. The others quieted down.

"Yes," Elizabeth continued. "We want to send you to Stoneybrook Academy. I have sent in your application."

"What?" I was horrified. Stoneybrook Academy is *my* school. I didn't want my pesky stepbrother in *my* grade with *my* friends. I looked at David Michael. It was hard to tell what he was thinking.

"Thanks, Mom," David Michael finally said. "But I like Stoneybrook Elementary. And I love being in Play-by-Play."

"We know," Elizabeth said. "But Stoneybrook Academy should be better for you. If you get in, you will receive more attention and you should do even better in class."

David Michael shrugged.

"Now *I* have a surprise for everyone," Daddy said. He put his fork down and cleared his throat. "This year we are going to spend Thanksgiving weekend in New York City."

"Yippee!" I shouted. Andrew and David Michael cheered. This was *great* news. Andrew and I were supposed to go to New York last year for Thanksgiving. But we did not.

"Will we see the parade?" I asked.

"Yes," Daddy answered. "We are going to stay in a hotel along the parade route. That way we can see the parade from our windows."

"Cool!" said Andrew.

"We have made reservations to eat a special Thanksgiving dinner in a restaurant," Elizabeth said.

"I have to phone the little house," I said. "I want to tell Mommy."

"You can call after dinner," said Daddy.

I was too excited to finish eating. But I did take a few bites.

Right after dinner Andrew and I called the little house. That is where Mommy and Seth live. (Seth is our stepfather.) Mommy answered the phone. She sounded happy to hear from us. She sounded even happier when we told her our news.

After we hung up, Andrew and I went upstairs to pack. Thanksgiving was only three weeks away. We wanted to be sure we were ready.

My Big Family

Remember I told you I had two houses?
Now I will tell you more about them.

When I was very little, Andrew and I
lived with Mommy and Daddy in one
house in Stoneybrook, Connecticut. Then
Mommy and Daddy started fighting — at
first a little, then a lot. Finally they got a
divorce. They told us they still loved Andrew and me very much, but they did not
love each other anymore. So Mommy
moved out of the big house. (It is the house
Daddy grew up in.) She moved to a little

11

house, not far away. Then Mommy married Seth. Daddy married again too. He married Elizabeth.

Here is who is in my little-house family: Mommy, Seth, Andrew, me, Rocky and Midgie (Seth's cat and dog), Emily Junior (my very own rat), and Bob (Andrew's hermit crab).

Here is who is in my big-house family: Daddy, Elizabeth, Kristy, Charlie, Sam, David Michael, Emily Michelle, Nannie, Andrew, me, Shannon, Boo-Boo, Goldfishie, Crystal Light the Second, Emily Junior, and Bob. (Emily Junior and Bob go back and forth when Andrew and I do.)

Kristy, Charlie, Sam, and David Michael are Elizabeth's children. (She was married once before too.) That makes them my stepsister and stepbrothers. Charlie and Sam are old. They go to high school. David Michael is seven like me. Kristy, as I told you, is one of my favorite people ever. She is thirteen and she runs a baby-sitting business with her friends from school. Emily

Michelle is my adopted sister. (I love her very much, so I named my pet rat after her.) Daddy and Elizabeth adopted her from the faraway country of Vietnam. Nannie is Elizabeth's mother. She helps take care of the big house and all us kids. The pets, too. We have a lot of them. Shannon is David Michael's puppy. Boo-Boo is Daddy's fat old cat. And Goldfishie and Crystal Light the Second are goldfish. They belong to Andrew and me.

I made up special nicknames for my brother and me. I call us Andrew Two-Two and Karen Two-Two. (I thought up those names after my teacher read a book to our class. It was called *Jacob Two-Two Meets the Hooded Fang*.) Andrew and I are two-twos because we have two of so many things. We have two houses and two families, two mommies, two daddies, two cats, and two dogs. Plus I have two bicycles, one at each house. (Andrew has two trikes.) I have two stuffed cats who look exactly alike. Goosie lives at the little house. Moosie stays at the big house. And we have two sets of clothes, books, and toys. This way we do not need to pack much when we go back and forth. I even have two pieces of Tickly, my special blanket.

I also have a best friend near each house. Hannie Papadakis lives near Daddy. Nancy Dawes lives next door to Mommy. Hannie, Nancy, and I are all in Ms. Colman's second-grade class at Stoneybrook Academy. We love Ms. Colman's class. (I hope David Michael does not end up in my classroom with my friends!)

Being a two-two is not too hard. Sometimes Andrew and I miss the family we are not staying with. But mostly we are very lucky. Think how many people can celebrate Thanksgiving with us!

4

Ms. Colman's
Second Grade

"Do you know what Linny did yesterday?" asked Hannie. (Linny is Hannie's brother.)

"What?" asked Nancy.

"First he was spying on me. Then he followed me all over the house. And he kept repeating everything I said."

I shook my head. "Brothers can really be pests," I said. (I was thinking of David Michael.)

The three of us were sitting on some desks in the back of the room talking, as we do every morning. We were waiting for Ms. Colman, our gigundoly wonderful teacher.

"Good morning, class," Ms. Colman said when she came in the room. "Please take your seats."

I hopped off the desk and went to sit in the front row. I have to sit there because I wear glasses. I sit next to Ricky Torres. He is another glasses-wearer. He is also my pretend husband. We were married on the playground at recess one day.

"Karen, would you please take attendance?" asked Ms. Colman.

"Sure," I answered. I love to take attendance. It is an important job.

I stood up and started checking off names in the attendance book. I put a check next to my name first. Then I checked off Hannie and Nancy because they are my best friends. I checked off Ricky and Natalie Springer. (Natalie also wears glasses. She sits in the front row, too.)

I checked off the twins, Terri and Tammy

Barkan. And Bobby Gianelli. (Bobby Gianelli used to be a bully, but he is not so bad anymore.) I checked off Pamela Harding, my best enemy, and her friends Jannie Gilbert and Leslie Morris. I checked off Addie Sidney. (She was moving her wheelchair away from our class computer and closer to her desk.) I checked off Chris Lamar, Hank Reubens, and Audrey Green.

I made a few more checks in the book and handed it back to Ms. Colman. Everyone was in class today, and that was good. I like my class just the way it is. We do not need any extra kids, especially not my stinky brother David Michael.

"Class, I have an important announcement to make," said Ms. Colman.

I sat up straighter. I love Ms. Colman's Surprising Announcements.

"Thanksgiving is only three weeks away," she said. "We are going to spend this month working on a special project. I want you to paint a big banner for the school's main hallway."

"Cool!" shouted Bobby.

"Please raise your hand, Bobby," said Ms. Colman. (Ms. Colman always has to remind Bobby not to call out in class.) "The banner will show the school what life was like for the early American settlers. It will be a big picture of a New England town more than two hundred years ago. To paint this banner, we will need to study how people dressed, what they did, what their houses and farms looked like, and what they ate."

Ricky raised his hand. "I want to study what they ate," he said.

"All right," said Ms. Colman. "I will be dividing the class into small groups of two or three people. Each group will study something different about the town. We will work on this project every afternoon after recess."

I raised my hand.

"Yes, Karen?"

"Can it be fall in this town?" I asked.

"Good question," said Ms. Colman. "Yes, it can."

Hurray! That meant I could draw lots of colorful leaves.

"Could we put a Thanksgiving feast in the picture?" asked Chris Lamar.

"Certainly," Ms. Colman replied. "You can draw feasts, houses, farms, schools, trees, animals, and people."

"What about trains?" asked Chris.

"There were no trains or cars then," said Ms. Colman. "That is why we will study the early American settlers first. We need to find out more about how they lived."

I could not wait to begin. We spent the next hour dividing into groups and deciding what to study. Hannie, Nancy, and I were in the same group. We like to do everything together. That is why we call ourselves the Three Musketeers. We decided to study what early schools were like.

I could not even imagine David Michael in *my* class with *my* friends.

Maybe David Michael could be in Mr. Berger's class. That was the other second-grade class in the school.

Ms. Colman's class was the best. I wanted to make sure it stayed that way.

5

Oink! Oink!

"Andrew, catch!" I called. I threw the red Frisbee high in the air. Andrew raced toward it. But Scott Hsu caught the Frisbee instead. (Scott and his brother, Timmy, live down the street from the big house. They often come over to play in Daddy's backyard.)

"No fair," said Andrew.

"The wind blew it right to me," said Scott.

"Can we play too?" Melody called from

across the street. Her brother, Bill, was with her.

"Sure," I answered. (I like playing with Melody. We are good friends.)

Soon Hannie and Linny came over too. We made a big circle and practiced throwing the Frisbee higher and higher. We were better at throwing than at catching. Then Scott grabbed a bunch of leaves and threw them at Timmy. Timmy grabbed an even bigger bunch and threw them at Scott. I threw leaves at Hannie. She threw some at Linny. Red, orange, and yellow leaves swirled through the air.

I was having so much fun, I did not see David Michael pull into the driveway with Charlie in the Junk Bucket. (That is what everyone calls Charlie's car.)

"Hey, David Michael's here!" shouted Bill. He raced to the car. So did Linny.

"Hi, guys! I just came from rehearsal," David Michael announced. "I have a very big part in the school play."

22

"Cool," said Bill.

"Yeah, guess what the part is," I said.

"What?" asked Linny.

"He plays Piglet. A *pig*." I made sure to say the word *pig* very clearly.

"You do?" asked Bill. He did not sound impressed.

"Yes," I said. "He has to learn to grunt and squeal and go 'Oink, oink.'"

Everyone laughed, except David Michael. He looked mad. He looked even madder when Scott and Timmy started yelling, "Oink, oink, oink." And when Hannie and Andrew began to snort.

"Pigs squeal, like this," I said. I performed some high-pitched squeals.

"Okay, Karen," said David Michael. His face looked a little red. "Why don't we play Frisbee?"

"Okay, Piglet. Anything you say," answered Bill. He grabbed the Frisbee and threw it toward David Michael. Linny joined them.

"Maybe we should pretend to be pigs," I shouted to the others, "to help David Michael with his part."

"Oink! Oink!" cried Scott. (I guess that meant he liked my idea.) Scott, Timmy, and Melody tumbled in the leaves, squealing and snorting.

I decided to make up a song. I sang to the rhythm of a rap tune I heard on the radio.

David Michael is a pig.
David Michael does a jig.
David Michael wears a wig.
Oink, oink, oink, oink, oink!

I thought my song was pretty good. The other kids joined in. Soon everyone, except David Michael, was singing. Even Bill and Linny. That made David Michael even more mad, since he is good friends with Bill and Linny.

"You guys are not funny!" cried David Michael.

"Yes we are," said Scott. "Oink, oink, oink, oink, oink."

"Karen, you started this. I am never talking to you again. Ever!" shouted David Michael.

Most of the other kids were too busy oinking and squealing to hear him. But I did. I did not care, though. I was having too much fun.

We kept oinking and squealing long after David Michael had gone inside.

6

David Michael: Major Pest!

David Michael meant what he said. At dinner he sat far away from me. "Kristy, could you pass me a roll . . . please?" asked David Michael. Kristy looked a little surprised. She was probably wondering why he was asking her, when the rolls were in front of me. She reached over my plate to grab the rolls. But not before I took one first.

"I do not want them now," David Michael said. "I do not want to eat anything Karen touches first."

27

"I do not want to eat anything you touch either." I bit into my roll. Daddy and Elizabeth told us to behave.

After dinner the phone rang. I rushed to answer it. It was Linny calling for David Michael.

"David Michael, telephone!" I yelled.

David Michael sat on the sofa in the family room. He was reading his *Winnie-the-Pooh* script. He did not even look up when I called him.

"David Michael," I said loudly. "It's Linny. Are you mad at him, too?"

"Karen, indoor voice," Daddy reminded me. (People are always telling me to keep my voice down.) David Michael turned a page of his script.

"David Michael," Daddy said, "you have a phone call from Linny."

"Okay," said David Michael as he walked to the phone.

"What a baby pig," I muttered.

"Karen." Daddy gave me a Look.

* * *

The next day David Michael, Kristy, and I sat at the kitchen table eating a snack. David Michael sat on one side of Kristy. I sat on the other. That way we did not have to sit next to each other.

"Do you guys want to talk about this?" Kristy asked.

"No," answered David Michael, looking at Kristy.

Just then, we heard the doorbell ring. I rushed to answer it. Scott and Bill were at the door.

"Oink, oink! David Michael, do you want to play ball with us?" said Scott. Bill squealed and oinked, too.

David Michael glared. I giggled. Kristy just looked.

On Friday morning I sat in the school lunchroom with Hannie, Nancy, and Addie. We decided to trade lunches.

I did not even look inside my Little Mermaid lunch box. I knew Nannie had packed me a good lunch. She always does. My lunch was probably better than anyone else's. The other kids must have thought so too, because everyone wanted to trade with me.

"Please, Karen," Nancy said. "You like tuna fish. I also have potato chips. And a homemade brownie."

Yummy. Nancy's mother makes great brownies. "Well, all right," I answered. I pretended I was doing her a favor.

I handed my lunch box to Nancy. She opened it — and gulped. "Oh, gross! I don't want to trade with you anymore, Karen. That was a dirty trick."

"What do you mean?" I grabbed the lunch box from her and looked inside. I gulped too. Inside were some bread crumbs and a moldy banana. Under the banana was a note:

Dear Karen,
    I was hungry. So, I ate some of your lunch. Pigs like to eat.

Oink, oink. Hope you like the ban-
nanna. I picked it out.

Piglet

I showed the note to my friends. "What
a pig!" exclaimed Hannie.

"Yeah. And he can not even spell *banana*," I said.

Nancy took her lunch back, but gave me
half her sandwich. Hannie gave me her
chocolate cookie, and Addie gave me her
apple. It helps to have good friends when
you have a pest for a stepbrother.

7

A Lecture

When I came home from school, I stormed into David Michael's room. "Why did you steal my lunch?" I shrieked. "You embarrassed me in front of all my friends!"

"*I* embarrassed *you*?"

"Yes. And you can not even write correctly." I put my hands on my hips. "Anyone in second grade should be able to spell *banana*."

David Michael put his hands on his hips, too. "Anyone in second grade should be able to spell *banana*," he repeated in a high-pitched voice.

"I do not sound like that," I said. I took my hands off my hips.

David Michael took his hands off his hips. "I do not sound like that," he repeated.

"Stop doing that!" I shouted.

"Stop doing that!" he shrieked.

I was so mad, I slammed his bedroom door and stomped into my room. I decided I would never, ever talk to David Michael again.

That did not stop me from slamming the kitchen door in David Michael's face the next time I saw him. I almost caught his pinky in the door. But luckily I did not. Even so, I got in trouble.

After David Michael tripped me in the hallway, Daddy and Elizabeth called us into the den.

"We are tired of all this fighting," Elizabeth said. "It is disrupting the whole house."

David Michael and I looked down at the floor. I sat on the comfy couch. David Michael sat in an armchair across the room. We wanted to be as far away from each other as possible.

"Fighting is not good for anyone," Daddy said. "I think you would both feel better if you would start talking to each other."

No way, I said to myself. David Michael scowled. Daddy sighed. "Look," he said. "I know you are both hurt — and upset. But all this teasing and fighting is only making you madder at each other."

"Karen started it. She told everyone I was a pig. And now whenever my friends see me, they oink."

I started giggling. "Karen," Daddy warned me.

"See what I mean?" said David Michael.

"All right. I can see you two are not ready to stop," Elizabeth said. She looked at us. "But you may want to make up soon. You may be in the same class at Stoneybrook Academy."

"Uugh," I groaned. I felt a little sick to my stomach. David Michael, in *my* class. That just could *not* happen.

David Michael looked surprised too.

"Yes," Elizabeth said, looking at David Michael. "I handed in your application papers. Soon you will spend a day at Stoneybrook Academy. In the morning you will take some tests. In the afternoon you will join a class so you can see what the school is like."

I hope he goes to Mr. Berger's class, I said to myself.

"You will probably join Karen's class for the afternoon," Elizabeth said, as if she had read my mind.

Boo and bullfrogs! I did not want David Michael in Ms. Colman's class for a whole afternoon. I did not want him in my class — ever.

8

Dungeons and Monkey Stew

In Ms. Colman's class Hannie, Nancy, and I were busy with our project. We were looking at books about growing up in colonial America. We even wrote to our pen pals in New York City. Their class was studying colonial America too. We wrote to them on our class computer.

My pen pal's name is Maxie Medvin. Here is the message I wrote to her:

Dear Maxie:
I think it is unfair that girls were not

allowed to go to school in colonial times. Why were boys so special?

Love,
Karen

P.S. I am sorry we will not be able to see you when we are in New York City. Maybe next time.

(Maxie's family was going to Vermont for Thanksgiving.)

About an hour later Maxie wrote back to me. Her class has a computer, too.

Dear Karen:

Some girls did go to school. They had private tutors or they went to private schools. It depended on their parents. Girls just were not allowed to go to public schools.

Love,
Maxie

Maxie's message made me feel a little better. I made Hannie and Nancy put some girls in the one-room schoolhouse we were drawing for the banner. "We can tell Ms. Colman it is a private school," I said.

Just then the final bell rang. Hannie and Nancy started putting away their scissors and crayons. Most of the other kids rushed out the door.

"Karen, may I see you a minute?" said Ms. Colman. I put my books into my backpack and walked to Ms. Colman's desk. (I hoped I was not in trouble.)

"Karen," Ms. Colman began, "David Michael will be visiting our classroom in two days. I am going to put an extra chair at your desk, so your brother can sit next to you."

Ms. Colman was smiling. She thought I would be happy. But I was not. "And," Ms. Colman said, "you will be in charge of taking David Michael on a tour of the school."

A tour? Yikes! This was sounding worse and worse. I looked down at the floor and muttered, "Okay. Um, see you tomorrow." Then I hurried out the door before Ms. Colman could see how mad I was.

As soon as David Michael came home from his rehearsal, I stormed into his room.

"You are coming to Stoneybrook Academy the day after tomorrow," I said.

David Michael was taking off his jacket. "I know," he said.

"Well, did you know that you are sitting next to me in class? And that I am in charge of taking you on a tour of the school?"

"Oh," David Michael said. He did not look too happy either.

"See you in two days," I said as I stormed out of his room. I flounced into my room and lay down on my bed.

"What am I going to do?" I asked Moosie. "I do not want my stinky brother sitting next to me for a whole afternoon. And I do not want to take him on a tour, either."

I could tell Moosie felt sorry for me.

Suddenly I had a brilliant idea. I was the only one taking David Michael on a tour. So I could make up all kinds of things about Stoneybrook Academy. He would never know the difference. I could make the school sound so awful, he would never want to go there.

I pulled Moosie onto my lap. "I could tell David Michael the school cook puts monkey eyes in the stew! I could tell him the stew is cooked with monkey meat. And that the school basement is haunted. And that it is really a dungeon. And that a one-eyed monster lives down there with two rats and lots of creepy, crawly spiders."

This was fun. I grabbed my notepad. I did not want to forget any details.

9

The Grand Tour

David Michael's big day at Stoneybrook Academy had arrived. We rode the school bus together. David Michael sat next to me. He did not even offer to change seats when I told him Hannie usually sits with me. This was not going to be a good day. I could tell already.

The guidance counselor, Mr. Perkins, met us at the bus. "Good morning, David Michael. Welcome to Stoneybrook Academy."

David Michael shook Mr. Perkins's hand.

I wanted to tell Mr. Perkins not to accept my dopey brother. But I did not.

"You will be taking some entrance tests this morning," Mr. Perkins explained to David Michael. "Then you will have lunch with your sister in the cafeteria."

I made a face. But Mr. Perkins did not see it. He led David Michael away.

David Michael sat next to me at lunch. Hannie and Nancy sat across from us.

"Mom gave me money to buy my lunch today," said David Michael. He headed for the lunch line.

"Um, David Michael, wait," I said. The cafeteria food at Stoneybrook was really good. If David Michael ate some, he would never believe my story about the monkey stew.

"Um," I repeated, "Nannie made me a big lunch today. Why don't we share?"

David Michael looked very suspicious.

"Really, it is a very good lunch," I said, handing him half a meatball sandwich, my grapes, and a homemade chocolate cupcake. (David Michael loves cupcakes.) "And you can save the money Elizabeth gave you for, um, costumes or something."

"Okay," said David Michael. He sat down again. Hannie and Nancy were giving me funny looks. They were probably wondering why I was being so nice to David Michael. But I could not explain. Not then, anyway.

At recess David Michael would not leave me alone. "You could play softball with Pamela, Chris, and Bobby," I hinted. I wanted some time with Hannie and Nancy — alone.

"I don't want to," answered David Michael.

"Well, you could go on the slides or the swings," I said, pointing to the swing set on the playground.

"No, I will just stay with you guys," said David Michael, smiling.

Grrr. He was driving me crazy.

* * *

After recess David Michael followed us into Ms. Colman's room. He sat with me at my desk.

Ms. Colman announced that we would work on the banner that afternoon. Yippee! Hannie, Nancy, and I were almost finished with our schoolhouse. Now we were drawing an outdoor scene, with lots of fall leaves and animals. I loved working on the banner.

"Karen," Ms. Colman called. "This would be a good time to give your brother a tour."

Boo and bullfrogs, I had almost forgotten about David Michael's school tour. "But what about the banner?" I asked.

"Hannie and Nancy can work on it until you come back," Ms. Colman answered.

"Okay," I muttered. I was not happy. But at least I could tell David Michael my made-up stories. I remembered to grab my note-pad before we left the room.

First I took David Michael to the library.

"You know," I began, "the librarian hates it when you borrow any fun books. She only wants kids to read encyclopedias and dictionaries."

"Really?" said David Michael. He was looking at Ms. Stanton, the librarian. She is actually very nice. I felt kind of bad making up stories about her.

Next we went to the cafeteria. "I've seen the lunchroom," said David Michael.

"I know you have," I said. (Didn't he think I remembered anything?) "But when we were eating, there were some things about the food I could not tell you."

"Like what?"

"Like how the cook puts monkey eyes and toad guts in the beef stew. And how — "

David Michael scowled. "You know, Karen," he interrupted. "I do not want to go to your stupid school."

"You don't?" This was news.

"No. I like my school. Most of my friends

47

go there. And I love Play-by-Play. You don't even have an after-school theater club."

I nodded. That was true.

"If I came here, I probably could not be in any more plays," said David Michael.

Hmm. If David Michael were not such a pain, I might try to help him stay at his old school.

Grandparents' Day

After recess one day, Ms. Colman wrote the word THANKSGIVING on the board in big letters.

"I can read that word," Bobby joked.

"I know all of you can read this word," Ms. Colman said. "But I want us to think about what this word really means. What are you thankful for?"

Pamela's hand shot up. "My new ice skates," she said.

Ms. Colman began writing a list on the board of all the things we said.

"VCRs," shouted Ricky.

"And in-line skates," said Leslie.

I thought about what I was really thankful for. My good friends Hannie and Nancy. I raised my hand. But Ms. Colman called on Nancy first.

"Friends," said Nancy, looking at me and Hannie.

"That is what I was going to say," I told Ms. Colman when she called on me. Ms. Colman underlined the word FRIENDS and smiled. The room became a little quieter. I guess everyone was thinking.

"I am thankful for a bed to sleep in," said Addie.

"And good food," said Bobby.

I raised my hand again. "I am thankful I can celebrate Thanksgiving with my family," I said. "Both my families." (My class knows about my two families.)

CELEBRATING WITH FAMILY, Ms. Colman wrote on the board. "Very good, class," she said. She looked proud of us. "But not everyone is lucky enough to be able to celebrate the holidays with their families. Many of our adopted grandparents at Stoneybrook Manor may be alone for Thanksgiving." (Stoneybrook Manor is where some senior citizens live. A few kids in the class adopted some of the residents as their grandparents. They visit them every week.)

"Grandma B will not be alone," Nancy announced. (Grandma B is Nancy's adopted grandmother.) "She's coming to dinner at our house."

"That is very nice, Nancy," Ms. Colman said. "But many of the other senior citizens will be alone. What should we do to cheer them up?"

Bobby remembered to raise his hand. "Let's take them out for pizza," he said.

"That is a good idea," Ms. Colman said. "But a lot of the people at the manor are on special diets. They may not be allowed to eat pizza."

Addie's hand flew up. "Maybe we could bring over some food the grandparents can eat," she suggested.

"Like turkey and cranberry sauce," added Ricky.

"Another good idea," said Ms. Colman. "But the cook at the manor is preparing a Thanksgiving feast for the people who live there."

Our class had more good ideas. Finally Hannie thought of the best one of all. We would invite our adopted grandparents to school for a party. They had never been to Stoneybrook Academy before.

Ms. Colman said we could have the party on the Tuesday before Thanksgiving. We would have the banner ready by then, so the grandparents could see it. We would also make invitations for the party and decorate the room. I could not wait.

11

Punch and Pumpkin Pie

"I think we should have lots of popcorn at our party," Pamela announced.

"And cake and cookies," added Bobby.

"All right," said Ms. Colman. "But we should have healthy food, too."

"But cookies are healthy," Bobby insisted. "At least the oatmeal-raisin ones my mother makes are." The rest of us laughed. We were having fun planning our Grandparents' Day party.

After a lot of talking, we thought of a very good party menu. Ms. Colman wrote our ideas on the blackboard. Here are some of the things we would be having:

1. Cupcakes. (I was going to make them, with Nannie's help.)

2. Oatmeal-raisin cookies. (Bobby and his mother would bake them.)

3. Pumpkin and apple pies. (Hannie's mother would bake them. Goody. Mrs. Papadakis makes wonderful pies.)

4. Popcorn and jelly beans. (Pamela and Omar said they would make popcorn and buy jelly beans.)

5. Sandwiches. (Chris, Ricky, and Addie said they would make them. I did not know Ricky likes to cook. But that is good. It is good to have a husband who cooks.)

6. Fruit salad. (Ms. Colman said she would make it herself. Yummy.)

7. Fruit punch. (Our class was going to make it the day of the party.)

Then Ms. Colman handed out construction paper, Magic Markers, crayons, stickers, glitter, scissors, and glue. "Class, I would like you to do two things. First, some of you need to make invitations for the residents at the manor. The rest of you can work on decorations. We need to brighten up the classroom for the party."

Yes! I love making decorations. Ms. Colman said we could make anything that reminded us of fall or Thanksgiving. Hannie cut out a chain of pumpkins. Nancy decorated an invitation for Grandma B. I decided to make a collage of fall leaves. First I drew big leaves on yellow, red, and orange construction paper. Then I cut them out and pasted them on a big sheet of blue paper.

"Now it looks like the leaves are falling against the sky," I said to Hannie.

While we worked, our class talked about what we would do at the party. Omar wanted to play games. Nancy wanted to dance. I wanted to sing. Addie wanted to write the grandparents a special poem.

"Those are all good ideas," Ms. Colman said. "But remember, a lot of the grandparents are very old. We do not want to tire them out with too many activities."

In the end, we decided to tell the grandparents about our banner. We would also sing some songs, dance (only if some of them wanted to), and eat. It was going to be a wonderful party.

Packing and Planning

It was already the Monday before Thanksgiving. I was very busy. I was packing for my trip to New York. I was also planning my outfit for our Grandparents' Day party the next day.

I could not decide between my red plaid dress or my blue velvet party dress. I put both dresses on the bed, along with a pile of T-shirts, all my favorite sweaters, my troll doll, and my pink plastic jewelry collection.

I reached under the bed for my suitcase. It felt kind of heavy. Then I remembered. I had already started packing.

I looked inside the suitcase. I found my favorite books, my camera, my notebook with the dinosaur on the cover, my Magic Markers, two pairs of sneakers, and my black patent-leather party shoes.

I started piling my clothes in the suitcase too. They did not all fit. I took out some books and my troll doll.

"Karen?" I turned to find David Michael staring at my suitcase. What did he want? "Aren't you packing an awful lot for just a few days?"

I scowled. "I might need all these clothes. I want to be prepared." (That reminded me. I still wanted to pack my ice skates and maybe my roller skates.)

"Oh," David Michael said. He even looked as if he understood. He had been nicer to me lately, ever since the neighborhood kids had stopped teasing him so much. I had actually been feeling a little better about him, too — ever since he told me he did not want to go to my school. But we were still fighting. "Nannie wants you to come to the kitchen," David Michael said. "Your cupcakes are almost ready."

Oops. I had almost forgotten about my cupcakes. David Michael followed me to the kitchen. He sat at the kitchen table memorizing his lines with Charlie.

Charlie: "Hello, Piglet. I thought you were out."
David Michael: "No, it's you who were out, Pooh."
Charlie: "So it was. I knew one of us was."
David Michael: "You know, I know Pooh's 'Tiddely Pom' song by heart."
Charlie: "Wait, that's not in the script."

"I know," said David Michael. "I'm just telling you. 'The more it SNOWS — tiddely-pom, the more it GOES tiddely-pom . . .' "

Big deal, I thought. I was tired of hearing about David Michael's play. That was all he ever talked about. I knew that his costume was almost finished, that he had his lines all memorized, and that his play was opening soon.

I shook sprinkles on my cupcakes to make them look extra fancy.

"May I have a cupcake?" asked David Michael when he finished singing.

"No," I answered. "They are for my class party tomorrow."

"Just one? I'll share it with you — and Charlie."

"No!" I shouted.

"Karen," said Nannie.

I sighed, and picked up the smallest, most lopsided cupcake. "Okay. You and Charlie may have this one," I said, handing

it to David Michael. Then I covered the other cupcakes and put them away. "I have to finish packing," I announced.

I went to find Kristy. Maybe she could help me decide what to wear.

13

Party Time

The next morning I was up very early. I did not want to be late for our class party. I put on my red plaid dress, white tights, and fancy party shoes. I found a red plastic necklace in my jewelry box and put that on, too.

I remembered to bring my cupcakes to school. I also remembered to carry the plate straight.

Everyone in class thought my cupcakes were beautiful. Even Pamela. And she is not always nice to me. (I am not always nice to her, either. We are best enemies.)

We were very busy before the grandparents arrived. We made fruit punch. We arranged all the food on a big folding table in front of the room. We blew up some orange, yellow, and red balloons. And we hung up our banner. (We were keeping the banner in our classroom for the party.)

I had just finished blowing up a big orange balloon when the grandparents arrived. Mrs. Fellows came in first. She works at the manor. Grandma B was right behind her. Grandma B does not even need a cane to walk. But many of the other grandparents do. Some even came in wheelchairs.

"Welcome to Stoneybrook Academy," Ms. Colman said after all the grandparents had sat down. "We are very pleased you could come to our party."

First we showed the grandparents our banner. Our class had drawn the coolest colonial town. It had a main street, a one-room schoolhouse, a meeting house, three churches, lots of farmhouses, dirt roads,

and horse-drawn buggies. The grandparents loved it.

Each group stood up to talk. I went first. (I wanted to.) I told the grandparents all about the one-room schoolhouse. Ricky asked if the grandparents had had to ride horses to school.

"No, we are not that old," one answered, laughing. "But I do remember buying milk from a horse-drawn cart."

"Really?" asked Ricky. His eyes grew rounder.

"Yes," said Grandma B. "And I remember when people used to cut ice out of Lake Michigan in the winter. We used that ice to keep our food cold in the icebox, before refrigerators were invented."

"Wow," I said.

Many of the other grandparents had old memories too. Our class loved listening to all of their stories. We were so busy talking, we almost forgot to eat. But Bobby reminded us.

Hannie and I helped Ms. Colman bring

punch and plates of food to some of the grandparents who could not walk very well. Pamela, Chris, and Omar showed the grandparents the computer. (Most of them had never used one before.) They were very impressed.

"Karen and Ricky, could you come here, please?" Ms. Colman called.

"Oops," Ricky whispered to me. "Are we in trouble?"

"I do not know," I answered. I brushed some pie crumbs off my skirt. I also checked to make sure I had not spilled punch on myself. What did Ms. Colman want?

Ricky and I walked slowly to where Ms. Colman was standing. "Children," Ms. Colman said, "some of the grandparents were not able to come to the party. I was wondering if you would help me pack up some of this food for them."

"Sure," we said. We made the plates of food look extra special. This was such a wonderful party, we were sad anyone had to miss it.

A Castle

"Oof," I said. I could not move my suitcase off the bed. Charlie had to carry it to the car.

"What do you have in here, Karen, rocks?" asked Charlie.

I shook my head. "No, I did not pack my rock collection," I answered. (I had thought about it, though.) I had not even packed my ice skates.

Everyone in my big-house family had a suitcase, even Emily Michelle. There were so many of us, we took the van *and* the car to the train station.

We all waited on the platform for the train to come. I was very excited. Soon I would be in New York City. (I love New York.)

Toot! Toot!

"Here comes the train," David Michael shouted. He was so excited, he jumped up — and landed on my big toe.

"Ouch," I cried. I gave him a dirty look.

"I didn't do it on purpose," said David Michael.

"I do not care. It hurts." I limped onto the train. Charlie carried my suitcase along with his.

The train was very crowded. We had to pile our suitcases on the overhead racks in two different train cars. And we could not find many seats together. I grabbed a seat across the aisle from Kristy. David Michael sat in another car with Nannie and Emily Michelle.

I tried to talk to the man next to me. But he was very busy reading a newspaper. So I looked out the window instead. I knew we were getting closer to New York when I saw tall brick buildings and sidewalks.

Suddenly the train went underground. I felt as if we were flying through a long dark tunnel. *Swoosh.* The train finally stopped.

"Grand Central Station," the conductor announced.

Everyone on the train started grabbing their coats and suitcases. People bumped into me. Or maybe I bumped into them. I was not sure. Kristy grabbed my hand and led me off the train.

Grand Central Station looked bigger and busier than ever. "Let's stay together," Daddy shouted above the roar of the crowd.

I could not stop looking up at the ceiling. Grand Central Station has a huge, high ceiling painted like the night sky.

Outside, Daddy and Elizabeth flagged down three yellow cabs. "Only four people can ride in each cab," Daddy said. "And there are ten of us."

"Yeah, and about a million bags," Sam added. (Sam is a big tease.)

"I do not want to ride with Karen," David Michael said.

"I do not want to ride with you, either," I said. Then I remembered my toe still hurt — sort of. I limped to the cab. Kristy and Elizabeth piled in behind me while the taxi driver put our suitcases in the trunk.

"Beckman Hotel, please," Elizabeth told the driver. And we were off. I looked at all the buildings, the crowds, the hot-dog stands, and the traffic. New York is a busy place.

The hotel elevator was made of wood, with gold buttons showing the floor numbers. Andrew and I could have ridden up and down the elevator all day. But Daddy and Elizabeth said we should go outside and enjoy New York while we were here.

I hurried to my room to put on my walking shoes. I was sharing my big, beautiful hotel room with Kristy, Nannie, and Emily Michelle. I felt sorry for Andrew. He had to share with stinky David Michael. (But at least Sam and Charlie were in his room too.)

When we were ready, we met Daddy and Elizabeth in the lobby. We crossed the street to go to Central Park. The park was full of people, dogs, strollers, and bicycles. We walked and walked, until we came to a pond.

"Look up," Daddy said, pointing.

We did. And I gasped. What was a castle doing in Central Park?

"That is Belvedere Castle," Daddy explained. "We can climb up to it."

We walked around the pond until we came to a stone staircase. Belvedere Castle was at the top of a high hill.

When we came to the top we could see that the castle rested on a big rocky ledge. It had towers and turrets and looked gigundoly cool. Everything in New York was.

15

The Parade

On Thanksgiving morning I was up early. So was everyone in my family. No one wanted to miss the parade.

First we had to have breakfast. Nannie and Elizabeth insisted. And they wanted to go out to eat.

Outside, people were already lining up behind wooden barricades to watch the parade. Policemen on horseback watched the crowd.

Andrew wanted to talk to one of the policemen. He wanted to ask him a million questions. Like do all policemen learn to ride horses? But Elizabeth and Daddy were in a hurry. We walked to a street called Broadway. (I knew that was famous.)

"I thought there were supposed to be theaters on Broadway," said David Michael.

"There are," answered Daddy. "But most of them are farther downtown."

"Look!" said Elizabeth. "There is Shakespeare and Company, a famous bookstore. And Zabar's. You can buy all kinds of food there." Zabar's was closed for Thanksgiving. But the coffee shop was not. (Thank goodness. I was hungry.)

I ordered a bagel with cream cheese. I did not want to ruin my appetite for Thanksgiving dinner. Charlie and Sam ate waffles — and pancakes, too. (Nothing ruins their appetites.)

On the way back to the hotel we saw even more people and policemen. I wanted to stay out on the street to watch the parade. But Daddy and Elizabeth said we could see it better from their bedroom window.

I could not believe I would finally see the Macy's Thanksgiving Day parade — in person. Already we could hear music from a marching band. But it sounded far away.

By the time we rode the elevator to Daddy's and Elizabeth's room, the band did not sound so far away anymore. Already I could see the band in their blue and white uniforms. We crowded around the windows.

"Look, there's a huge balloon of the Cat in the Hat," Andrew shouted.

"Cool," I said. (I love the Cat in the Hat. And he looked as tall as a building.)

"Oh, there is the first float," I shrieked. (No one even told me to keep my voice down. They were all too excited.)

The float was shaped like a turkey. People dressed in feathers stood on top of the turkey and waved to the crowd.

We saw floats decorated like snowflakes, hearts, and St. Bernards. There was even a

movie float with strips of film all over it and a giant projector. (I loved that float. I want to be a famous movie star someday.)

We saw marching policemen, marching firemen, marching bands, and marching choirs.

But my favorite things in the parade were the balloons. "There is Donald Duck," I shouted.

"And Betty Boop," said Charlie.

"And Woody Woodpecker and Clifford," said Andrew.

"Cifford! Cifford!" shouted Emily Michelle. (She loves Clifford the Big Red Dog.)

"Oh, and there is the Santa float," Sam said. I saw Santa waving in his sleigh, led by eight white (pretend) reindeer.

"The Santa float is always last," Elizabeth said.

"To remind people Christmas is coming," Daddy added.

I was sad the parade had ended. "It was great, wasn't it?" I asked my family. I did not wait for an answer. I knew it had been the best parade ever.

Un Deux Trois

"Ew, my dress is wrinkled," I said.

"Emily Michelle, please give me back my lipstick," cried Nannie.

"Oh, no, I have a hole in my tights," said Kristy.

We were very busy after the parade. We were dressing for our special Thanksgiving dinner.

I put on my blue velvet dress, lacy white tights, and black patent-leather shoes. (The dress did not look too wrinkled after I put it on.) Kristy found another pair of tights. Soon we were ready.

Daddy asked the hotel doorman to hail three cabs. The doorman opened the cab door for me. I felt like a lovely lady sitting between Daddy and Kristy.

"One twenty-three West Forty-fourth Street," Daddy said to the driver.

"Where are we going?" I asked.

"To a restaurant called Un Deux Trois. That's French for One Two Three," said Daddy.

"Oh," I said. I was a little worried. What if the waiters did not understand English? What if the cook did not know how to make turkey?

"Karen," Daddy began. (I guess he could see I looked worried.) "Un Deux Trois has a special Thanksgiving menu today, with turkey, stuffing, and all the trimmings. It's a fun restaurant."

Daddy was right. Un Deux Trois turned out to be gigundoly cool. It had big chandeliers hanging from the ceiling, and walls the color of butter. Best of all, there were cups full of crayons at every table, and paper tablecloths we could draw on!

As soon as I sat down, I started drawing a picture on the paper in front of me. I drew myself standing on the movie float, waving to the crowd in a long red dress, just like a real movie star. David Michael was drawing something too. But I could not see what it was. He was sitting too far away.

Most of us ordered the Thanksgiving special: turkey with cranberry sauce and stuffing, mashed potatoes, yams, zucchini, creamed onions, and corn bread. (Boy, that sounded like a lot of food.) When the waiter asked me what I wanted to drink, I answered in French.

"Vous lait bebee, oui oui, non, issi."

The waiter did not understand my pretend French.

"She would like milk, please," Daddy told him.

"Wee, wee!" Emily shouted while we waited for our food.

"Non, non!" cried Andrew even more loudly.

"Andrew, Emily, please settle down," said Daddy.

Emily started blowing bubbles in her milk with her straw. Andrew poked me in the arm with his spoon.

"Stop it," I said.

Nannie cleared her throat. "Why don't we each describe something we are thankful for?" she suggested. "Andrew, since you're so wiggly, you may go first."

"Um," Andrew began, "I am thankful for my red sneakers."

Sam said he was thankful for the new girl in his class named Suzanne. Kristy rolled her eyes. "Oh, please," she said.

It was Daddy's turn next. He looked around the table before he answered. "I am thankful for my health," he answered.

I was thankful for Daddy's health too. He

had a heart attack last year. But he was better now, thank goodness.

"I am thankful my family is around me this Thanksgiving," said Nannie. Then she looked at me. "You know, one of my friends just lost her brother," Nannie continued. "Imagine the sad Thanksgiving she must be having."

Yipes, I thought. It must be awful to lose a brother. I could not imagine my life without Andrew, Sam, Charlie. Or David Michael.

I had to admit, I would really miss David Michael if anything happened to him. I hoped nothing ever would.

I looked at David Michael. He was wolfing down some rolls the waiter had just brought to our table. He looked the same as always. I waved to him, but he ignored me. Some things never change.

17

A Truce?

It was Sunday. We had been home for a whole day. And I had hardly seen David Michael at all. (Except at dinner, when he sat at the other end of the table.)

"Nannie, have you seen David Michael?" I asked.

Nannie looked up from her baking. "No," she answered.

"Daddy, where is David Michael?"

Daddy looked at me over his newspaper. "I don't know, Karen."

"Charlie, do you know where David Michael is?"

Charlie finished tying his shoelaces. "No. I haven't seen him all morning."

I sighed. Ever since Thanksgiving dinner, I had decided to be nicer to David Michael. I was sick of fighting with him. But David Michael was still mad at me. He would not talk to me much in New York. And on the train ride home, when I offered him my seat, he sat in another car. (Boo and bull-frogs.)

I finally found David Michael sorting through the mail. He looked kind of nervous.

"Hello," I said.

"Oh, hi," answered David Michael. He did not look too happy to see me.

"What are you doing?"

"I want to see if there's a letter from Stoneybrook Academy."

"Oh," I answered. That made sense. "Is there one?"

"No, but it should come soon."

Poor David Michael. He was very worried about having to change schools.

On Monday I came right home from school. I did not even meet Hannie in the backyard. I wanted to see if David Michael had heard anything from Stoneybrook Academy.

"The mail has not come yet, Karen," Nannie said.

Suddenly David Michael rushed through the door. "Guess what," he said to Nannie, Emily Michelle, Sam, and me.

"What?" I asked.

"Heather, the girl playing Winnie-the-Pooh, had to drop out of the play," David Michael began. "And I have her part — the lead. I just can't switch schools now."

"So who is going to play Piglet?" I asked.

"Another boy who knows that part. But I am the only one besides Heather who knows Pooh's part," said David Michael.

Just then Kristy came in with the mail.

"No letter from Stoneybrook Academy," she announced.

David Michael looked only a little relieved. "It will come soon," he said.

After dinner I decided to talk to David Michael alone. I found him in his room, studying his lines.

"Uh, David Michael," I began.

David Michael looked up from his script. He seemed surprised to see me.

"I'm really glad about your new part in the play," I said.

"Me too," said David Michael. He looked down at his script again.

"Um," I said. "Look, I am tired of being mad at you."

David Michael looked up. "You are?"

"Yes. And I want to help you stay at your old school."

"You do?"

"Yes. I have an idea."

18

An Idea

My idea was very simple. "All you have to do," I told David Michael, "is talk to Daddy and your mom. You have never told them you do not want to go to Stoneybrook Academy. You should at least do that."

"But will they listen to me? They love Stoneybrook Academy. They really want me to go there."

"You have to try to make them understand. Just talk to them."

"I don't know," said David Michael, shaking his head.

I sighed. "I will go with you," I said. "Why don't we talk to them right now?"

David Michael just looked at me. "Okay," he finally said, putting down his script.

We found Daddy and Elizabeth in the den.

"We have something to tell you," I blurted out. Then I gave David Michael a look that said, *Talk.*

"Um," David Michael began. "You know . . . uh, Mom and Watson . . ."

"Just tell them the way you told me," I suggested.

David Michael took a deep breath. "I just wanted to tell you I do not want to change schools. I really like Stoneybrook Elementary. All my friends are there."

Daddy and Elizabeth looked very surprised. "You don't want to go to Stoneybrook Academy?" Elizabeth repeated.

"No," David Michael said. "Especially not now. I do not want to give up the lead in *Winnie-the-Pooh.*"

"Yes, and you know how much David Michael loves acting," I said.

Daddy nodded. He looked thoughtful.

"If I changed schools," David Michael said, "I could not be in Play-by-Play anymore."

"But your schoolwork would improve more at Stoneybrook Academy," said Elizabeth.

"He has been doing better and better at his own school all fall," I said.

"Hmm," said Elizabeth. "We thought David Michael could improve even more at Stoneybrook Academy. But maybe he could stay at Stoneybrook Elementary and we could find a tutor for him."

"Really?" asked David Michael. His eyes shone.

"Really," said Elizabeth.

I could not resist giving David Michael the thumbs-up sign.

"In any case," Daddy said, "we will put off making any decision until after Christmas. That way David Michael can star in his play. And we will all have a chance to think this matter over more carefully."

Elizabeth nodded. "And we will talk to David Michael before we make any final decisions."

"Cool," said David Michael. "Thank you." He looked relieved.

"Thank you, Karen," said David Michael as we walked back upstairs. "Thanks for helping me talk to Mom and Watson about this."

"It was nothing," I said modestly. "Can we be friends now? I am tired of all this fighting."

"I am too," said David Michael. "I guess I was jealous because you always do so well in school. And I was having so much trouble."

Wow. I had never heard David Michael admit that before.

"But," David Michael said, "I was really mad when you made so much fun of me for playing Piglet."

"I'm sorry," I said. "I know that was mean. I guess I was jealous of you too. Everyone is so proud of you. I sometimes feel left out, since Andrew and I do not always live here."

David Michael nodded. "Yeah," he said. He looked as if he really understood.

"You know," I said, smiling, "I might want to be an actress when I grow up."

David Michael smiled too. "Would you like to help me practice Pooh's lines?"

"Sure," I answered.

19

Opening Night

It was the opening night of David Michael's play. Andrew and I were at the little house with Mommy and Seth. But Mommy said I could still go to the play with my big-house family.

I was very excited. Charlie and Kristy were picking me up in the Junk Bucket. And I was all ready.

Ding-dong.

"Kristy and Charlie are here," I called to my little-house family. I rushed to open the door.

Mommy, Seth, and Andrew stood on the steps and waved good-bye to us. (Andrew was not going to the play because it ended way after his bedtime.)

"Tell David Michael to break a leg," Mommy called.

"Mommy, what do you mean?" I asked.

"That means wish him good luck," Seth explained. "It's what people say in the theater."

"Oh," I said.

The play was being performed in the auditorium at David Michael's school. When we arrived, the parking lot was full. So was the auditorium.

"Mom and Watson are sitting near the front," Kristy said. "They are saving seats for us."

"Thank goodness," I said. I did not see many empty seats. Luckily, we found my big-house family. Everyone was there except Emily Michelle (and the pets, of course).

"Who is staying with Emily?" I asked.

"Stacey," answered Kristy. (Stacey is in the Baby-sitters Club with Kristy. She is very nice.)

I started reading my program. "Look how big David Michael's name is," I whispered loudly.

"Shh, Karen, the play is about to start," said Kristy.

The lights dimmed and the curtain rose.

David Michael was the first one onstage. He wore a light brown wool bear costume, and he sang:

The more it snows
        (Tiddely pom),
The more it goes
        (Tiddely pom) . . .

Cool. It looked as if real snow were falling.

Soon Piglet, Eeyore, and Christopher Robin came onstage too. Piglet's costume was shiny and pink, but he did not look very funny. He just looked like a pig (which

was how he was supposed to look).

I was proud of David Michael. He spoke clearly. He never mixed up his lines. (Piglet did.) And he sang better than anyone else.

When the curtain went down, I clapped and clapped for David Michael. He had to bow four times before the audience stopped clapping. I saw Nannie and Elizabeth trying not to cry. (Why do grown-ups cry when they are happy?)

We met David Michael after the show. He was still wearing his Pooh costume. Daddy patted him on the back. Elizabeth hugged him. Then I hugged him, too.

"You were really good," I said. "Gigundoly good."

20

Snow and Stars

Right after David Michael's show, it began snowing. Two nights later, it was snowing again. I sat in my room reading *The Boxcar Children*. It was about four orphans who lived all by themselves in a boxcar in the woods.

"I wonder what the Boxcar Children do when it snows this much?" I asked Goosie.

"Karen, telephone!" Mommy called.

"Coming!" I called back.

"Hello?" I said when I picked up the phone.

"Hello, Karen. It's David Michael. The letter from Stoneybrook Academy arrived."

"What does it say? What does it say?" I shrieked.

"I've been accepted into third grade, beginning next fall."

"Are you going to go?"

"No. I do not think so. I talked to Mom and Watson. I am going to work with a tutor at Stoneybrook Elementary. If I keep my grades up, they said I could stay at my school."

"Great!" Even though David Michael and I were friends now, I was still relieved he was not going to be in my class.

"I'm really happy," said David Michael. "Now I do not have to worry about leaving Play-by-Play. You know, we are putting on *The Wind in the Willows* next. I am going to try out for the part of Toad."

I muffled a giggle. I imagined David Michael with a big head, no neck, bulging eyes, and webbed feet. "I really hope you get the part," I said.

"Thanks, Karen," said David Michael. We talked a little more. It felt good to be friends again.

I put down the phone and walked back to my room. But I was too excited to keep reading. Christmas was coming. I wanted to make David Michael a special present. Maybe I could make him a Christmas-tree ornament in the shape of a star. After all, he was the star of his play.

Someday I might be a star, too. And David Michael and I could star on Broadway — together!

About the Author

ANN M. MARTIN lives in New York City and loves animals, especially cats. She has two cats of her own, Gussie and Woody.

Other books by Ann M. Martin that you might enjoy are *Stage Fright*; *Me and Katie (the Pest)*; and the books in *The Baby-sitters Club* series.

Ann likes ice cream and *I Love Lucy*. And she has her own little sister, whose name is Jane.

Little Sister

Don't miss #80

KAREN'S CHRISTMAS TREE

The fight was still going on when the school bell rang at the end of the day.

I let Nancy get on the bus first. Then I found a seat far away from her. I did not have much else to do on the ride home, so I started to worry. I worried about our holiday plans. What would we do about the Wish Tree? What would we do about the Druckers' new blue-spruce tree? What would we do about giving holiday presents to each other?

The more I thought, the more miserable I felt. The holidays were coming and instead of having two good friends to celebrate with, I had two ex-friends who were not talking to me.

Boo-hoo-hoo and bullfrogs.

LITTLE 🍎 APPLE™

BABY SITTERS®
Little Sister

by Ann M. Martin,
author of The Baby-sitters Club ®

More Titles... ➡

The Baby-sitters Little Sister titles continued...

- -

Available wherever you buy books, or use this order form.

Scholastic Inc., P.O. Box 7502, 2931 E. McCarty Street, Jefferson City, MO 65102

Please send me the books I have checked above. I am enclosing $ _____
(please add $2.00 to cover shipping and handling). Send check or money order – no
cash or C.O.Ds please.

Name _____ Birthdate _____

Address _____

City _____ State/Zip _____

Please allow four to six weeks for delivery. Offer good in U.S.A. only. Sorry, mail orders are not
available to residents to Canada. Prices subject to change.   BLS596